W9-AOM-058

Poseidon and the Sea of Fury

DON'T MISS THE OTHER ADVENTURES
IN THE HEROES IN TRAINING SERIES!

Zeus and the
Thunderbolt of Doom

HEROES IN TRAINING

Poseidon and the Sea of Fury

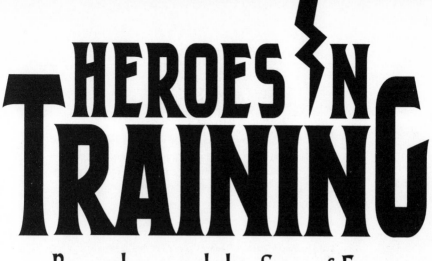

Joan Holub and
Suzanne Williams

Aladdin

NEW YORK LONDON TORONTO SYDNEY NEW DELHI

This book is a work of fiction. Any references to historical events, real people, or real places are used fictitiously. Other names, characters, places, and events are products of the authors' imagination, and any resemblance to actual events or places or persons, living or dead, is entirely coincidental.

ALADDIN

An imprint of Simon & Schuster Children's Publishing Division
1230 Avenue of the Americas, New York, NY 10020
First Aladdin hardcover edition December 2012
Text copyright © 2012 by Joan Holub and Suzanne Williams
Illustrations copyright © 2012 by Craig Phillips
All rights reserved, including the right of reproduction in whole or in part in any form.
ALADDIN is a trademark of Simon & Schuster, Inc., and related logo is a registered trademark of Simon & Schuster, Inc.
Also available in an Aladdin paperback edition.
For information about special discounts for bulk purchases, please contact Simon & Schuster Special Sales at 1-866-506-1949 or business@simonandschuster.com.
The Simon & Schuster Speakers Bureau can bring authors to your live event. For more information or to book an event contact the Simon & Schuster Speakers Bureau at 1-866-248-3049 or visit our website at www.simonspeakers.com.
Designed by Karin Paprocki
The text of this book was set in Adobe Garamond Pro.
The illustrations for this book were rendered digitally.
Manufactured in the United States of America 1112 FFG
2 4 6 8 10 9 7 5 3 1
Library of Congress Control Number 2012947276
ISBN 978-1-4424-5798-0 (hc)
ISBN 978-1-4424-5265-7 (pbk)
ISBN 978-1-4424-5266-4 (eBook)

For our heroic husbands:

Mark Williams
—S. W.

George Hallowell
—J. H.

⚡ Contents ⚡

Greetings, Mortal Readers,

I am Pythia, the Oracle of Delphi, in Greece. I have the power to see the future. Hear my prophecy:

Ahead, I see dancers lurking. Wait—make that *danger* lurking. (The future can be blurry, especially when my eyeglasses are foggy.)

Anyhoo, beware! Titan giants now rule all of Earth's domains—oceans, mountains, forests, and the depths of the Underwear. Oops—make that *Underworld*. Led by King Cronus, they are out to destroy us all!

Yet I foresee hope. A band of rightful rulers called Olympians will arise. Though their size and youth are no match for the Titans, they will be giant in heart, mind, and spirit. They await their leader—a very special, yet clueless godboy. One who is destined to become king of the gods and ruler of the heavens.

If he is brave enough.

And if he accepts that sometimes he must share the cage—um—*stage* with fiends. Oops. *Friends!*

For only by working together will these young rulers-to-be have a chance at saving the world.

CHAPTER ONE

Under Attack!

A SPEAR WHIZZED BY TEN-YEAR-OLD Zeus's ear. He ducked his head but didn't stop running. Neither did his two companions, Hera and Poseidon. They were right behind him.

"Halt in your tracks or you're dead meat, Snackboy!" a cruel voice boomed.

He'd know that voice anywhere. It was Lion Tattoo. That was what Zeus had nicknamed him, anyway. He was the leader of the three half-giants who were after Zeus. They were soldiers in King Cronus's army and stood as tall as trees.

Just three days before, they'd snatched Zeus from his cave in Crete and brought him here to Greece. He'd already escaped them—twice. But he might not be so lucky a third time.

"When we catch you, we *will* eat you!" hollered a second voice. Blackbeard's. Another of the half-giants.

Then the third one—Zeus had dubbed him Double Chin—added his two cents. "Yeah! And we'll chomp your friends for dessert! Ha-ha-ha!" He followed this up with a loud burp.

A shiver ran down Zeus's spine. They were probably bluffing, though. Their orders were more likely to take him, Hera, and Poseidon back to King Cronus. So that the *king* could swallow them whole!

They approached a ditch. Zeus jumped in and hunkered down, waiting for Hera and Poseidon to catch up. Within seconds Hera dropped in to crouch beside him.

"We'll never reach the sea at this rate. Somebody else is going to find that trident thingie before we do. Do something, Thunderboy!" she hissed.

Zeus liked the nickname she'd given him. But she sure did know how to make it sound like an insult sometimes.

"Don't be so impatient. We'll get there," he told her. "We're on a quest, remember? You can't expect it to be fast or easy."

An oracle named Pythia had sent them on this quest to search for a magical trident. Which was going to be a challenge, since none of them knew what a trident was. But they did know their destination—the sea.

Just then Poseidon dove between them, thumping their shoulders as he fell.

"Ow!" Zeus and Hera complained at the same time.

"Half-giant soldiers? This is all we need," Poseidon complained back. "My feet are killing me."

Zeus's were too. No wonder. In the past two days they'd journeyed over hills, across valleys, and through forests.

Hera rolled her eyes at Poseidon. "Wuss."

"I am *not* a wuss!" he objected. "I'm an Olympian."

"Well, then act like one," Hera snapped.

"What makes you the boss of how Olympians act?" Poseidon snapped back.

"I'm an Olympian too, remember?" said Hera. "You don't hear *me* whining."

"Would you two stop arguing for half a second?" Zeus pleaded. "Those soldiers are going to hear you." Hera and Poseidon had been fighting almost the entire trip!

"I don't hear anything," Poseidon whispered a few minutes later. "Think we lost them?"

Hera peeked out of the ditch. "The coast looks clear. So what now?" They both looked at Zeus.

Zeus lifted the amulet that was strung on a leather cord around his neck. He'd found it at the temple in Delphi. He studied the amulet, a chip of rock about the size of his fist.

"Which way?" he asked it.

The strange black symbols on the chip's smooth, gray surface began to move around. Acting like a compass, they formed an arrow pointing east.

"That way," Zeus told the others. Hopping out of the ditch, he was off again. Hera and Poseidon followed.

But no sooner had all three left their hidey-hole than another spear whizzed over their heads. *"Yeeoch!"* It came so close it nearly parted Zeus's dark hair.

"Fee, fi, fo, fum. Look out, Snacklets. Here we come!" *Stomp, stomp, stomp.* It was the unmistakable sound of half-giant sandals pounding toward them.

"They're baaack!" shouted Zeus. He and Hera took off, running neck and neck.

Poseidon surged past them. His turquoise eyes were round with fear. And he seemed to have forgotten all about his feet hurting.

Hearing a *caw* overhead, Zeus glanced up. A seagull circled above them. He pointed at it. "We must," he said, panting, "be getting close to the sea."

He was right. Around the next bend in the road, they spotted the Aegean Sea off to their left. It was bright blue and dotted with little islands. Weird, wispy steam rose from its surface. Its waters churned and bubbled.

Zeus recalled the oracle's words—words that had prompted their quest and led them to this sea: *Trouble, trouble, boil, and bubble! You must find the trident. One that will point the way to those you seek. One that—in the right hands—has the power to defeat the first of the king's Creatures of Chaos.*

Hera glanced down at the sea as she ran. "I hope we make it that far," she said breathlessly.

Just then a sharp electric jolt zapped Zeus in the ribs. "Ow!" he yelled. But the jolt reminded him that he *did* have a weapon to use against the soldiers.

"You guys keep going!" he called to Hera. "I'll catch up later!"

"Okay!" Hera's long, golden hair whipped in the wind as she kept running.

Zeus slowed, reaching for his zigzag dagger. It was tucked under the belt at his waist. He freed it, then spoke a command. "Large!"

With a sound like the crunching of a glacier, the bolt expanded. In an instant it became a glowing thunderbolt as tall as Zeus. It sparked and sizzled with electric energy.

Grasping it tightly, Zeus drew it back. Then he sent it soaring. "Zap them, Bolt!" Immediately the thunderbolt took off after Hera and Poseidon.

"No! Not *them*," Zeus called in the nick of time. "The Cronies!" That was what everyone called King Cronus's soldiers. Not to their faces, though, because they didn't like it one bit.

The bolt screeched to a halt in midair. Then it switched directions and buzzed off toward the soldiers. Zeus ran the other way to catch up with Hera and Poseidon. He would have to be

more exact in his commands from now on. He'd nearly fried his friends!

Zzzpt! "Ow!" *Zzzpt!* "Ow!" The air behind him was soon filled with yelps and curses. Bolt was zapping one soldier after another.

Then Lion Tattoo's voice rang out, "Retreat!"

CHAPTER TWO

Sea Journey

ZEUS LAUGHED AS THE SOUND OF THE half-giants' stomping sandals grew distant. "Ha! Take that!" he yelled. Lion Tattoo pretended to be fierce, but he'd been afraid of a little bee back at Zeus's cave on Crete. A thunderbolt must seem a hundred times more terrifying to him.

Zeus jogged down the steep, rocky hillside. Below him fishermen were mending nets on the shore. Hera and Poseidon were there too, waiting on a dock overlooking the sea.

Zeus could hear the roar and crash of waves as he moved lower. This was one angry sea!

Just as he reached the beach, his thunderbolt zoomed back. Shrinking to dagger size, it slid into place beneath his belt.

"Good boy, Bolt," Zeus told it. Happy little sparks sizzled from between his fingers as he gave it a pat. The thunderbolt glowed with pride.

To think that he'd once been desperate to get rid of it! He'd found it stuck in a huge cone-shaped stone on display at the temple in Delphi. It was the same temple where he'd first met Pythia, the oracle.

After he'd pulled the thunderbolt out, it had stuck to his hand like glue. He had tried everything to get rid of it. Nothing had worked.

He'd had a good reason for not wanting to

keep it. It *scared* him. He'd been struck by lightning dozens of times back on Crete, and it wasn't fun. But now that he'd realized Bolt wasn't out to zap him, they were getting to be, well, friends. It was a little worrisome.

"Don't get too attached to me," he warned the bolt. "Because you're not really mine. Pythia said you belong to some guy named Goose. He's destined to become king of the Olympians."

After crossing the beach, Zeus stepped off the sand onto the wooden dock. Being king of the Olympians wasn't a job he'd want. This Goose guy was going to have his hands full—whenever Zeus found him. After all, Hera and Poseidon were Olympians. Ruling over them would be a pain in the butt!

"Soldiers gone?" Poseidon asked as Zeus came up to him and Hera. The three of them eyed the hillside where they'd been attacked.

"For now, anyway," Zeus replied. "But more will come."

"Then let's get out of here," Hera said impatiently. "Any idea where to start looking for this so-called trident?"

At her question the chip amulet around Zeus's neck twitched. He looked down at it. The black symbols had formed a new arrow. This one pointed straight off the end of the dock toward the sea. Zeus held the amulet up so Hera and Poseidon could see it too.

"So we're supposed to dive into the sea? And just start randomly searching?" Hera asked skeptically.

Poseidon's eyes went wide. "No," he said, backing away. "I can't swim! And if I fall into seawater, I'll—I'll melt!"

Hera frowned. "Wuss," she taunted. "It's pointing to the sea. We have to go."

Zeus held his ears. He wasn't used to so much blabbering. Until three days ago he'd lived a boring life in his quiet cave on Crete with a silent nymph, a bee, and a goat.

"Did you fight like this the whole time you were in the king's belly?" Zeus asked with a frown. But his companions were arguing too loudly to hear him. He sometimes couldn't help wondering if freeing them had been a mistake!

He could still picture how surprised King Cronus had looked when Zeus had thrown his thunderbolt down the king's throat. How the giant Titan king's face had turned red as he'd choked. And then green as he'd barfed up Poseidon, Hera, and three more Olympians— two girls and a boy.

Zeus couldn't remember the names of those three now. They had been quickly recaptured by King Cronus and his Titan buddies.

The bickering slowed, and Zeus let go of his ears. He was just in time to hear a tiny voice pipe up. "Hip-sip," it said.

Startled, Hera and Poseidon jumped. Then they stared at the amulet, since that's where the voice had come from. "Did that thing just talk?" Hera asked.

Zeus nodded. "Guess I forgot to tell you it does that."

"'Hip-sip'?" said Poseidon. "What's that mean?"

"It's Chip Latin," Zeus explained. "Like Pig Latin. Only, you move the first letter of a word to the end and add an 'ip' sound instead. As in 'chip.'"

"So 'hip-sip' means *'ship'*!" Hera exclaimed. "Where can we get one?" She looked at the amulet as if waiting for a reply. But the chip of stone was silent.

Zeus shrugged. "Guess we're supposed to figure that part out on our own."

"Oh." A look of intense concentration came over Hera's face. She squeezed her forehead with her fingertips.

"What are you doing?" Zeus asked.

"Trying to use my magic powers to get us a ship. If you can command a magic thunderbolt, it must mean Poseidon and I can do magic too. After all, we're all O— Ow!"

Poseidon had just elbowed her sharply, shaking his head.

"We're all what?" asked Zeus, looking from one to the other of them.

"Nothing," she said, looking away.

"Hera and I don't know for sure that we have magic powers," Poseidon explained. "All we know is that King Cronus fears us. And the others."

The other three Olympians who'd been in Cronus's belly, he meant. Who knew where they were now.

"He may fear you," Zeus said, "but I think he fears *me*, too. Just wish I knew why."

Hera and Poseidon traded secretive looks. Before Zeus could open his mouth to ask what *that* was all about, a fisherman came by. "Looking for transport?" he asked them.

When they nodded, he led them to a small sailing ship about ten feet long. "It washed up onshore this morning," he told them. "No one's claimed it, so you're welcome to it. But you're crazy if you go out in these rough seas. I've never seen them this angry."

"Look at the name painted on the side!" said Poseidon, pointing to the boat. "No way. I'm not getting into a boat named *Sinker*!" He backed away.

Zeus peered more closely at the painted lettering. "Wait! There's a *t* that's faded out. So it's not named *Sinker*; it's—"

"Stinker?" finished Hera doubtfully. "Oh, much better."

Zeus didn't like to rush into things, so he walked around the boat, studying it. It looked a bit leaky, but it would have to do.

They thanked the fisherman and bid him good-bye. Then they shoved the *Stinker* into the water and hopped aboard.

And they were off. Into the furious sea!

CHAPTER THREE

Fiiissshh

ANYBODY KNOW HOW TO STEER A
boat?" Zeus asked once they'd set sail.

Poseidon didn't answer. Struck dumb
with terror, he was gazing at the steaming, boiling sea around them.

"I'm sure I can figure it out," said Hera,
brimming with confidence. She stood to go to
the tiller, a lever used to turn the boat. "Yikes!"

She stumbled when a wave knocked them unexpectedly. Then she toppled over the side!

"She'll be boiled alive!" Poseidon shrieked.

When she bobbed to the surface again, Zeus grabbed her arm. He and Poseidon reeled her back into the boat.

"Weird," Hera said once she was inside. "The water's not that hot, even though it's boiling."

"Hmm. Maybe its fury is just meant to scare people off," said Zeus. "To keep them away from the sea, so they won't come searching for the trident."

Taking the tiller, he figured out the basics of sailing after a few tries. To go in the direction the chip amulet pointed, he actually had to move the tiller the opposite direction.

Hera and Poseidon managed to angle the sail into the wind. Soon they were speeding over the choppy sea.

"I feel seasick," Poseidon complained after a while.

"Then hang your head over the side of the ship!" Hera said in alarm.

Poseidon leaned over the ship's bow and threw up. "Hey, I feel a lot better now," he said after he straightened again. "In fact, I'm hungry."

"Me too," said Zeus. His stomach was growling. Except for a few apples they'd snatched from an orchard that morning, they hadn't eaten all day.

Hera looked at Zeus. "The sea must be full of fish. Maybe you could spear one with your thunderbolt?"

Zeus put a protective hand over Bolt. He stared at Hera in horror. "Are you kidding? If this thunderbolt gets wet, it could electrocute us all!"

Hera was smart about some things. But she obviously didn't know that lightning and water don't mix.

Poseidon licked his lips. "Fiiissshh," he said dreamily. He stretched his arms out in front of him. "I wish I could catch one right now."

To everyone's astonishment, a huge silver fish suddenly leaped out of the water. *Thump!* It landed neatly in Poseidon's outstretched arms. He staggered backward under its weight.

"Whoa!" Zeus caught hold of Poseidon's tunic before he could topple overboard too.

"Fiddling fishscales! That was close," said Poseidon. He gazed at the water with renewed fear.

After Zeus broiled the fish with his thunderbolt, the three ate their fill. "Yum!" Poseidon pronounced, licking his fingers. "I could eat seafood every day of the week."

"It's good," said Hera, "but I wouldn't eat it *every* day."

"Me? I'm on a seafood diet," said Zeus. "When I see food, I eat it!"

The three of them laughed. For the first time since meeting the two Olympians, Zeus almost felt like they could become friends. But then again, maybe he only felt that way because his belly was full. And because no one was chasing them. Not at the moment, anyway.

Little did he know that this peace wouldn't last long.

Keeping an eye on the direction the amulet's arrow was pointing, Zeus adjusted the tiller. The Aegean Sea continued to boil and bubble. The wind blew steadily as they forged ahead.

And then they began to see the shipwrecks. Dozens of them. Ships, dinghies, sailboats—all dashed upon the rocky islands they passed. The sea's fury had done this!

"Tell me about the other Olympians," Zeus suggested. He wanted to keep them all from thinking about the possibility that they might accidentally wind up wrecked too. "The ones that were with you in King Cronus's belly. What were their names again?"

"Hestia, Demeter, and Hades," said Hera. "Girl, girl, boy," she added in case the names were unfamiliar to him.

Zeus nodded. "I still don't get why Cronus swallowed all of you, though."

"Duh. To keep us imprisoned," said Poseidon.

"Because he fears your magic powers?" Zeus asked. "But why does he think they're dangerous to him? I mean, you don't even know what they are, much less how to use them."

Hera and Poseidon exchanged a guarded look.

"All right," Zeus said. "What's the big secret?" Before they'd started their journey, Hera had said she had one, but she wouldn't tell him what it was. Because she suspected he might be one of Cronus's spies!

"Look," he said. "I helped you escape. What more proof do you need that I'm on your side?"

"The trident," Hera said stubbornly.

Poseidon nodded.

Zeus opened his mouth to argue.

"Shh!" Poseidon interrupted. "Do you hear that?"

Zeus and Hera cocked their heads to listen too. The sound of harp music and beautiful singing filled the air.

"I wonder where it's coming from," Zeus said. He peered through the veil of steam.

"Over there!" Poseidon said excitedly. He pointed toward a tiny island surrounded by jagged rocks and cliffs.

Suddenly Zeus didn't care about finding the trident anymore. He just wanted to get near the music.

"Let's go in for a closer look," Poseidon suggested.

"Great idea," said Zeus. He shifted the tiller, turning the ship toward the island. The arrow on the chip amulet was pointing in the opposite direction, but he ignored it.

The steam slowly lifted. There were three women perched on the rocks! They were dressed in flowing robes and had wings.

As the three women strummed their harps and sang, Zeus was filled with an intense longing for family. For the parents he'd never known. They'd abandoned him in the cave. Why?

Somehow he felt that these women could tell him. *We have all the answers,* their song seemed to say.

Hera pointed to Zeus's amulet. "Stop! Chip wants us to turn around."

Zeus looked down. The amulet's arrow was

glowing red now. It flashed on and off pointing them *away* from the island. Still Zeus ignored it and steered directly for the rocks.

"Got to get closer," he murmured.

"Must. Listen. Forever," Poseidon added in a dreamy voice.

"What's wrong with you?" Hera asked, looking between them worriedly. She snapped her fingers in Zeus's face, but he didn't even blink. And Poseidon seemed just as far gone.

"I think those women and their rock music have put you both under a magic spell!" she said. "Only, for some reason it's not affecting me."

As if in a trance, Zeus steered the *Stinker* even closer. "Anger-dip!" shrieked the chip. Which meant "danger." But Zeus paid no attention. His head was full of music.

All at once the song changed and sounded more sinister. A huge wave swelled behind them. It began pushing the ship straight for the jagged rocks.

The song ended. The women started cackling.

"Look out!" screamed Hera. "We're going to crash!"

CHAPTER FOUR

Sea Serpents and Merpeople

SUDDENLY THE BOAT GAVE A HARD JERK.
Zeus and Poseidon bumped heads.
"Ow!" They exclaimed at the same
time. Freed from the song's spell, Zeus shook
his head dizzily. He felt like he'd just awak-
ened from a dream. One that had turned into
a nightmare!

He and Poseidon sprang into action, trying to
help Hera get control of the ship. It creaked and

groaned as the giant wave pushed it. The rocks loomed closer. And closer.

Just as the *Stinker* was about to be splintered into toothpicks, two sea serpents rose from the water. They were as big as half-giants and had tails twice the length of the sailboat.

One of the serpents curled its scaly blue-green tail under the ship and tossed it high. The other did an expert twist. With a flip of his tail, he batted the boat away from the rocks.

"Hold on!" yelled Zeus as the *Stinker* went whirling through the air. Seconds later it splashed down so hard that it nearly fell apart. But somehow it landed upright and intact, with the three of them still safely inside.

Hera got up from the bottom of the boat where she'd fallen. "Why did you listen to those singers?" she demanded.

"Um," Zeus said.

"Uh, well," said Poseidon.

The two sea serpents overheard and swam up to them. "Don't blame yourselves. Those were Sirens," one of them said. "Their beautiful music lures sailors to their deaths. *Boy* sailors, that is."

"So there," Poseidon said to Hera. "They put us under a magic spell."

"Yeah, we couldn't help it," said Zeus.

"Whatever." Hera's eyes flicked to the sea serpents. Before anyone could thank them for their good deed, they dipped their heads in a farewell bow. Then they turned and glided off.

"Did you see how those serpents were staring at me?" Poseidon asked. "It was like they knew me or something."

"What? You're crazy," scoffed Hera. "They were looking at all of us."

"Maybe," said Zeus. But it seemed to him

that they really might've been staring extra hard at Poseidon. *Strange.*

Poseidon shivered. "Well, the sooner we find that trident thing and get out of this creepy sea, the better."

"Agreed." Zeus checked the chip's arrow, which was black again. Then he moved the tiller to take them in the right direction.

Night fell and they sailed on. Two more sunless days and starless nights passed. They took turns sleeping and manning the tiller and the sail.

When it rained, they collected fresh water in a bucket they'd found onboard. And every time they grew hungry, Poseidon had only to say, "I wish for fish." Immediately a fish would leap into his arms.

"Why don't you try wishing for something else to leap into your arms next time?" Hera suggested to him one morning. "Like a trident."

Poseidon nodded. "I already thought of that.

Only it didn't work." His eyes got big as he stared at something beyond Zeus. *"Flipping fish-heads!* Who are they?"

Zeus looked in the direction Poseidon was gazing. Three heads were peeking up over the ship's stern. They giggled in what sounded like children's voices. But they weren't children. One had a beard. And they all had turquoise eyes like Poseidon's.

"So it's true," the bearded one said. He was staring at Poseidon in awe. "The sea serpents told us you would come one day. We've waited a long time. Have you come to rescue the sea?"

Poseidon blinked. "Who, me?"

"Who are you?" Hera asked them.

"Not exactly," Zeus answered. They'd all spoken at the same time.

"We're merpeople," replied one of the creatures. The three of them were now swimming gracefully around the ship.

"Well, we're here to search for a trident," Zeus told him. "Have you seen one?"

"Sure. Got one right here." The bearded merman held up a three-pronged spear. It looked sort of like a pitchfork, only cooler.

Zeus's eyes lit up. Could it be this easy? Had they already found the magic trident?

But then the other two held up tridents of their own. "Every merperson has one," said a mergirl with long pink hair.

"Is there a special one somewhere, though?" Zeus asked.

All three merpeople nodded. "Oceanus has the mightiest of them all," said the merman. "Fearsome what it can do!"

"Where can we find him?" Zeus asked quickly.

The merpeople huddled close, looking scared at the very idea. "You must not get around much. Where are you from?" the merman asked.

"Belly," Hera and Poseidon said together before Zeus could answer.

The merpeople glanced at Poseidon, appearing intrigued.

Zeus shrugged. "Cave," he said. It was hard to learn much when you were raised in places like that, but they were trying to make up for lost time.

The merman zoomed backward on his tail, then dove with a splash. When he came up again, he said, "Oceanus pretty much rules the sea. He could be anywhere in it."

"Is he a friend of King Cronus's?" asked Hera.

The merpeople looked even more fearful at the mention of the king. "Probably," the mergirl told them. "Those twelve Titans usually stick together."

"Oceanus is a Titan?" gasped Hera.

"Twelve!" Zeus echoed. He'd only seen *six* Titans that night he'd met Cronus.

It seemed pretty clear to him that Oceanus's

trident must be the one they sought. But just how they were going to get it from a Titan, he had no idea. If they told him Pythia wanted them to have it, would he just hand it over? Not likely!

"Where can we find him?" Zeus asked again.

"*You* don't find *him*," the merman said. "*He* finds *you*. If you're very unlucky, that is."

The younger green-haired mergirl nodded. "Instead of looking for him, you should turn around and sail as far south as possible."

"Because that's where he lives?" asked Poseidon.

The merpeople sent him another strange look. Then they giggled again.

"No," said the merman. "Because it's the best way to avoid being buried at sea."

Hera glared at Poseidon. "I think they mean we go north to find him, Doofus-eidon."

CHAPTER FIVE

Trident Trouble

HOW DO WE KNOW FOR SURE IT'S Oceanus's trident we're after?" Hera argued as Zeus steered their boat north.

He tacked left and their boat sped over the waves. "You heard what the merman said. It's fearsome and mighty. It *must* be magic."

If he didn't know any better, he'd think Hera was scared to meet Oceanus. But then, why wouldn't she be? Titans were bad news. Still, getting the trident was the whole point of their quest!

Hera frowned. "Pythia didn't actually *say* that the trident is magical. She just said it will *point the way to those we seek.* 'To the lost Olympians' is what she meant."

Or to my parents, Zeus thought. Finding them was his constant hope, even though he had no idea who or where his parents were.

"Maybe one trident is as good as another," Hera went on. "I think we should go back and find those merpeople again. They seemed friendly. I bet one of them would let us borrow a trident."

Poseidon grinned at Hera. "Cluck, cluck," he said, flapping his arms like wings. "I think someone's chickening out."

"Am not!" Hera protested hotly. Balling her

hands into fists, she stomped toward Poseidon, rocking the ship.

"Stop! I told you I'll melt if I fall into the water!" he squealed.

"Promise?" Hera countered with a too-sweet smile. But she left him alone and sat down.

"Let's think this out," Zeus said, hoping to stop their fighting. "Pythia said the trident has the power to defeat the first of the king's Creatures of Chaos. Don't you think a trident powerful enough to do that would have to be magical?"

"I'd think so," Poseidon said smugly.

"Maybe," said Hera. "But she said the trident only has power if it's *in the right hands*. What if my hands are the right ones? Maybe *I* can use one of the merpeople's tridents to defeat these so-called Creatures of Chaos—whatever they are."

"So go back," suggested Poseidon. He grinned at Zeus. "We won't stop her, will we?"

"It's Oceanus's trident we want," Zeus said. "I'm almost sure of it."

Hera crossed her arms. "Look, Mr. Bossy Thunderpants. I demand that you turn this boat around and go find those merpeople."

Zeus couldn't believe her nerve. And she thought *he* was bossy! "We'll lose time if we backtrack now," he told her. The wind was blowing steadily, and they'd already left the merpeople far behind. "I say we go on."

Hera glared at him. "And I say—"

"Look! Dolphins!" interrupted Poseidon, pointing off to the right. A pod of them were leaping in the waves. Their slick silver sides flashed as they dove and then resurfaced.

He sent Hera a mischievous look. "I think you should catch a ride back with one of them.

Then Zeus and I could have some peace." No sooner had the words left his mouth, than one of the dolphins headed toward them.

Zeus, Hera, and Poseidon watched in amazement as it drew up alongside the ship. Fixing an eye on Hera, it chattered at her as if inviting her onto its back.

"See?" said Hera. "This proves I'm right to go back. Even that dolphin knows it!"

The dolphin kept on chattering, but now it was eyeing Poseidon. "Don't look at me," he said, sitting down. "I'm staying put."

But Hera climbed over the side of the boat and straddled the dolphin's back. "As soon as I have the trident, I'll come find you," she told the boys. "If Oceanus doesn't find you first. I mean, you might be hard to locate if you're fish food at the bottom of the sea."

"Gee, thanks," said Poseidon.

"And what if you're wrong?" Zeus asked. "What if it turns out that the merpeople's tridents have no powers at all?"

Hera shrugged. "What if it turns out Oceanus's trident doesn't have any? I guess we'll find out who's right soon enough." She clutched the dolphin's dorsal fin with one hand and sent them a confident wave of farewell. Obviously she figured she was going to be right.

"Bye, then," said Zeus.

"Later," said Poseidon. "Lots of cluck—I mean *luck*."

Before the dolphin zipped off across the water, it looked up at Poseidon and winked.

"Whoa!" said Poseidon as it swam off. "Did you see that?"

Zeus nodded. "First the sea serpents, then the merpeople. And now the dolphin. For someone

 51

who's scared of the sea, you have an odd effect on its creatures."

"What did you see when those Sirens called to us?" Poseidon asked out of the blue.

"What did *you* see?" Zeus hedged, embarrassed to say.

Poseidon's eyes shifted away. He looked a little embarrassed too. "Nothing. It was dumb. Let's just go."

With the wind filling the ship's sails, they sped north. It was more peaceful now that Hera was gone. Zeus's ears enjoyed the quiet, but he kind of missed her.

Still, he was pretty sure he and Poseidon were on the right track. And that Hera was on the wrong one. After all, the arrow on his stone amulet had pointed steadily north all day. Chip wanted them to go that way.

As they sailed on, the sea grew even angrier,

rocking them from side to side. Huge bubbles broke the surface of the water as it roiled and boiled. The surf sizzled and splashed against the rocky shores of islands they passed. Shores with even more shipwrecks.

Zeus checked his amulet. The arrow had changed from black to red and was spinning around in circles. *Huh?*

"I think we're here," he said.

Poseidon looked around nervously. "So where's Oceanus?"

Without warning, a giant golden claw-hand rose from the sea. It lifted the *Stinker* above the water. Then it flung the boat away in a high arc.

One minute they were zooming through the air. The next, they were falling!

"Hang on!" Zeus yelled. Thinking fast, he grabbed the thunderbolt from his belt. If it fell

into the sea, he and Poseidon could fry.

With all his strength Zeus hurled the bolt. "Fly to the closest island!" he commanded. Bolt zoomed off.

In the very next instant Zeus and Poseidon were dashed under the waves of an angry sea.

CHAPTER SIX

In Hot Water

"ZEUS, WHERE ARE YOU?" IT WAS Poseidon's voice.

Treading deep underwater, Zeus could barely hear him. He looked up. Their ship was directly above him. It hadn't sunk! He kicked his feet and shot to the surface of the water. Poseidon was sitting on the boat, which was now floating upside down.

"Here I am," Zeus gasped. "And you didn't melt after all!"

"Yeah, well, I could've drowned, though," Poseidon said. Quickly he changed the subject. "Think that was Oceanus just now?"

"If it was, he's in a bad mood. Let's get to land," Zeus said, pointing toward the nearest island. "I have to find Bolt. And I think the boat might need repairs."

One of their oars came floating by, and he nabbed it. Then Poseidon reached out an arm and helped pull him from the water.

Sitting atop the overturned *Stinker*, Zeus rowed toward shore. The wild, boiling sea fought them all the way, tossing them about. At any moment they might sink.

"We're going nowhere fast," Poseidon said. He slid into the water behind the boat. With powerful kicks he propelled it forward faster than Zeus could even paddle.

"Thought you said you couldn't swim!" Zeus said in surprise.

"Guess I was wrong," Poseidon said, sounding surprised too.

They'd only gone a dozen yards when Zeus heard an odd clacking noise. Thinking he had water in his ears, he tilted his head to one side.

From behind him Poseidon asked, "Um, Zeus? Do you think that, besides his clawed hands, Oceanus has lots of muscles? And maybe a long beard?"

"How would I know?" asked Zeus. "I've never seen him. Unless he was in the forest with the other Titans the night I rescued you from King Cronus."

The clacking sound had grown louder.

Strange. Zeus tipped his head to the other side in case the water was in his other ear.

"I wonder if Oceanus also has horns on top of his head," Poseidon went on. "Horns that look like crab claws."

"Horns like crab claws?" Zeus laughed at the idea.

"WHAT'S SO FUNNY ABOUT CRAB CLAW HORNS?" boomed a voice.

Zeus whirled around so fast, he nearly toppled over. There, swimming beyond Poseidon, was a muscular, bearded giant. One with claw hands, who also had two big crab claws growing from the top of his head! The claws were all angrily clacking together.

"Oceanus?" Zeus squeaked the question.

"That's my name. Don't wear it out," the Titan declared. His skin was golden, and his long, thick serpentine tail floated behind him in a loose coil.

"Uh, okay," Zeus said.

"Well? State your business!" Oceanus commanded. *Clack, clack, clackety-clack!* went his claws, like he was just itching to pinch somebody.

Zeus wished Poseidon would speak up. Why should *he* have to do all the talking? He glanced toward the end of the boat, where Poseidon had been. He'd disappeared! That coward. Was he hiding under the boat?

"Well?" Oceanus prodded. He glided closer.

"Pythia sent us," Zeus explained, paddling faster. If he could get to the island and find Bolt, he'd have a weapon to use against this crazy claw guy. "She's this oracle in Delphi. And according to her prophecy—"

Oceanus frowned, his bushy green eyebrows forming a V. Slowly he rose from the sea until he rode the water with his tail.

"I'm supposed to find a magical trident," Zeus rushed on. "If you'd let me borrow yours, maybe I could use it to calm the sea, and—"

"WHAT?" The Titan's golden face turned purple with rage. "HOW DARE YOU! I made these seas furious—and furious they will stay."

Rearing back, he uncoiled his tail. It whipped toward Zeus, ready to lash him. Zeus ducked, sure he was a goner.

But before the Titan's tail could strike, Poseidon popped up in the water. Right between Oceanus and Zeus. Reaching up with one hand, Poseidon knocked the tail away. It seemed to cost him little more effort than swatting a fly.

Zeus stared in amazement. Oceanus's tail had to weigh a ton!

As Oceanus tried to right himself, Poseidon swam to Zeus. "I've seen it!" he exclaimed in hushed excitement.

"Seen what?" asked Zeus. He was still thinking about what had just happened. Did being in water somehow give Poseidon superstrength?

"The trident," Poseidon said. "He's got it strapped to his side like a sword. It's all gold and glittery. Way more magnificent than that merman's trident."

All too quickly Oceanus recovered from the shock of having his tail shoved aside by a puny Olympian. He gave chase, zooming smoothly through the water toward them. Since his back was to the Titan, Poseidon didn't notice.

"Watch out!" Zeus warned.

Poseidon whirled to face Oceanus. "Give me the trident, you overgrown snaky crustacean," the boy commanded. "It's mine!"

"Shh! Are you crazy?" Zeus hissed. "Oceanus will send us both to a watery grave! Besides, what makes you think the trident is meant for you?"

Before Poseidon could reply, Oceanus bellowed at them. "Overgrown snaky crustacean, am I?" *Whap!* His powerful tail uncoiled and smacked the water.

"Nyah, nyah. Missed me!" Poseidon yelled back. "You don't deserve that trident. You've been using it for evil instead of for good."

Suddenly Zeus caught on. Poseidon was trying to goad Oceanus into *using* his trident. Because until it was freed from his side, they had no hope of grabbing it away from him.

"Hey, Fishbreath!" Zeus called out to Oceanus. "I bet your trident is only a fake. I bet it doesn't have any powers at all. It's probably not even real gold!"

"Fake? I'll show you how *not* fake it is!" Oceanus roared. All at once the trident flashed golden in his fist. He pointed its three-pronged tip at the water. As he drew the trident upward, the water followed. It was like he'd raked the ocean into a towering wave!

Uh-oh, thought Zeus. But it was too late to take back his taunts.

Just before the wave crashed down, Zeus saw Poseidon dive beneath the water. Then the wave hit, and Zeus was lost in a swirling whirlpool.

CHAPTER SEVEN
On the Island

L UCKILY, THE GIGANTIC WAVE DIDN'T do Zeus in. But it did wash him and the *Stinker* all the way to the shore of a nearby island.

Standing on the beach, he looked out to sea. Thunderation! Unfortunately, he couldn't see anything through the rising steam. He could hear Oceanus and Poseidon battling it out, though. *Splash!*

"Ow!"

"Take that!"

He wanted to be out there too! At the Delphi temple in Greece, Pythia had called him a hero in training. But a true hero would be in the sea right now, helping Poseidon fight Oceanus.

Zeus righted the boat. Then he pushed it back into the water and hopped in. *P.U.!* It stunk inside. Clumps of rotting seaweed had gotten twisted around its broken mast. "*Stinker*" really was a good name for the boat now.

Its sail was in rags, and its broken mast was useless. He started to paddle, but soon the boat began leaking. It had a hole in the bottom the size of his fist! No way would he make it without repairs. He turned around and dragged the *Stinker* back onto the beach.

Then he rushed inland to look for something to plug the hole. Up ahead in an outcropping of rock, he saw something sparking.

"Bolt! Is that you?" he called. The sparking grew brighter and more frantic. Running over, Zeus found the thunderbolt stuck in a boulder, tip first.

"Calm down," he soothed. He grabbed it with both hands and wrenched it out of the rock. It was easy—like pulling a knife from a block of cheese.

"If *I* can do this so easily, why couldn't you get loose on your own?" he wondered aloud. "For the same reason you couldn't get out of that cone-stone back in Pythia's temple? Maybe certain kinds of rock are like thunderbolt traps, huh?"

The thunderbolt didn't answer, of course. But once it was free, it darted here and there. It did flips and pinwheels in the air around him, glowing and sparking.

"Happy to see me?" Zeus asked, laughing.

He tugged his belt away from his waist, making a space. "Small!" he instructed. Instantly Bolt shrank to dagger size, dove for his belt, and slid under it. Then the thunderbolt went still.

Zeus got back to business, hunting for sap, reeds, and bits of wood. His thoughts were racing. Now that he had Bolt, he could use it to fight Oceanus. But though his aim was improving with every throw, he couldn't risk hurling Bolt over the water. He might electrocute every creature in the whole sea. Including Poseidon.

Swimming was out too. He wasn't that good at it. Not like Poseidon had turned out to be. No, his only hope was to fix the boat. And fast!

He ran back to the *Stinker* and flipped it over. Then he plugged the hole in its bottom with the stuff he'd collected.

Out at sea the battle raged on. *Clack-clack!*

Splash! "Ow!" Now and then Zeus caught flashes of the golden trident through the steam.

Minutes later the boat was ready. By rocking it back and forth, Zeus managed to turn it upright again.

Just as he launched, the entire sea quieted. The steam began to clear. Was the battle over? Where were Oceanus and Poseidon? Who had won?

Zeus paddled out in the boat, his heart pounding with worry. He gazed in all directions across the water. It was eerily calm and empty.

"Poseidon!" he called. No answer. His panic multiplied. What if Poseidon was dead?

But then, not more than twenty yards away, Poseidon's head popped up out of the water. Another head popped up too. It wasn't Oceanus's, though. It was another boy's.

Poseidon held the golden trident high in

triumph. Its glittery length flashed in the sun-light. "Yes! I beat him!"

Then he pushed the trident underwater. The two boys straddled its long handle. Suddenly they were zooming across the sea toward Zeus fifty times faster than he could paddle. *Whoa!*

Poseidon drew up beside the boat. "Zeus, meet Hades," he said, idling the trident just enough to keep it afloat. "Found him at the bottom of the sea. Oceanus was under orders from Cronus to keep Hades prisoner there."

The new boy shook the water from his dark, curly hair, then stared at Zeus. "I remember you. You're the one who freed us from Cronus's belly, right? Thanks for nothing," he said in a gloomy-sounding voice.

"Hey!" Zeus protested. "What's that supposed to mean?"

"It means I liked it in that belly," Hades

informed him. "It was better than being held captive undersea. It's cold down there!"

"Sorry," Zeus said, feeling kind of annoyed. Talk about ungrateful!

"Oceanus had Hades locked inside a big air bubble so he could breathe. He couldn't escape it without drowning," Poseidon explained. He did a few fancy zigzag turns on the trident. One hard turn sent a fan of water spraying over Zeus. "Oops. Sorry." Poseidon came to an abrupt stop.

"Watch it!" Zeus protested, brushing seawater from his eyes.

"Yeah. This trident is magic, you know," Hades warned Poseidon. "Be careful."

Poseidon just shrugged, acting cool. Winning a battle against a sea god had made him a little bit full of himself. Zeus couldn't blame him, though. It was a pretty epic victory.

"You wouldn't believe the great palace Oceanus

has got," Poseidon told Zeus. "It's way down deep. Tons of rooms. All carved out of coral. Shells and pearls everywhere. The guy is rich!" He was zooming around the boat in tight circles now.

Zeus stared at him, a little jealous. "You got all the way down to the bottom of the sea?" There was no way he could ever swim deep enough to see this fabulous palace. "How did you hold your breath for so long?"

"I don't know," said Poseidon. "It was like I didn't need to breathe. Weird, huh?"

I'll say, thought Zeus. Suddenly it all clicked together. Poseidon's not needing to breathe in water. His new strength and swimming ability. Fish giving themselves up whenever he was hungry. The way the sea serpents, merpeople, and that dolphin had stared at him.

The creatures of the sea had recognized Poseidon as their leader! The trident really was intended for him. Poseidon's hands were *the right hands.*

"Um, can we go? Oceanus is still down there," Hades said nervously. "Caught in his own net, thanks to Poseidon. But I doubt it'll hold him for long. We should scram, and quick."

Zeus shuddered at the thought of Oceanus escaping again. Those claws of his looked sharp. "Once he does get free, he'll come after his trident," Zeus said. "And *us.* I say we take him captive now, while we have the upper hand."

Hades went pale at the suggestion.

"No way! Are you bonkers?" asked Poseidon.

"He's a Titan, isn't he?" Zeus argued. "If he gets out of that net, he'll go right back to helping King Cronus again. Wouldn't it be smarter to find some kind of prison and take him there while he's tied up?"

Honestly, thought Zeus, *didn't they get it?*

The trident might be rightfully Poseidon's. And Poseidon could swim ten times better than him. But *Zeus* had ten times more *brains*.

"I don't want to be anywhere around him if he gets loose from that net," Hades warned. "One flip of his tail, and—" He drew a finger across his throat.

"Anyway, how would we carry him to a prison?" Poseidon added. "He's too big to fit in the boat or on the trident."

"Well, what do you guys suggest, then?" Zeus asked.

"Run!" yelled Hades. He was staring at something in the distance, his eyes wide.

Zeus shook his head. "That won't help." But then he stopped talking as he heard an all-too-familiar sound.

Clackety-clack-clack!

CHAPTER EIGHT

Titan Transport

OCEANUS WAS ON THE LOOSE AGAIN! HE was still mostly trapped in the net, but he'd poked his head and tail free. And now he was zooming toward them, muscles bulging and claws clacking.

Poseidon spun the trident so Zeus could climb onto the end of its handle behind Hades. "Hurry! Get on!"

Once all three boys were atop the trident,

Poseidon cut across the water. Instead of fleeing, though, he headed straight for Oceanus!

"Turn! Turn!" Zeus and Hades begged.

Poseidon ignored them. They got closer and closer to the Titan. It looked like they were going to ram him!

At the last minute Zeus ripped the thunderbolt from his belt and tossed it high. "Hover!" he commanded, hoping it would obey.

Fearing for their lives, he and Hades both jumped off the trident. *Splash! Splash!*

As Zeus watched Poseidon ride onward, he saw that Oceanus had slowed his approach. The Titan began to back away. Something had scared him. Was it Poseidon? Suddenly Oceanus turned tail and dove, making a break for it.

Poseidon leaped from the trident, still clutching it in one fist. As his feet hit the water, they turned scaly. So did his legs. He'd sprouted a fish tail! "Wa-hoo!" he shouted. "Is this the coolest, or what?"

He slapped the surface of the water with his new tail. He twirled the tip of it overhead. Slick rainbow-colored scales glittered in the sunlight.

Zeus and Hades swam in closer. "Awesome tail!" Hades called out.

"Admire it later!" Zeus hollered. "What about Oceanus?"

"Chill out," Poseidon said. "I'm going fishing. I'll snag that Titan in no time. Just watch me." Balancing his new tail on the surface of the water, he poked the three-pronged end of the trident into the sea. In the exact spot where Oceanus had disappeared.

"Long!" he commanded. Instantly the trident began to lengthen in the water. It extended deeper and deeper. It could change size like Bolt! Speaking of Bolt, Zeus looked up. The thunderbolt had obeyed him and was hovering high overhead. *Phew.*

Poseidon began raking the trident back and forth. Minutes later he smiled big. "Gotcha!"

As Poseidon reeled Oceanus in, Zeus and Hades treaded water nearby. By the time the Titan reached the surface, the trident's handle had shortened itself again.

Oceanus glowered at the boys as he tried to wriggle loose from the net. But though his head and tail were free, his arms and torso were still tangled in it. The net was made of tough stuff. Though Oceanus tried to cut through it with his claws, he couldn't do it. "RELEASE ME AT ONCE!" he demanded.

"Not gonna happen," said Poseidon. He sprang from the sea and landed on Oceanus's back. The instant Poseidon left the water, his tail turned back into legs. He scrambled upward, scaling the sturdy net.

The Titan twisted around. His claws reached for Poseidon, trying to pinch him through the net. But Poseidon dodged them. When he reached Oceanus's shoulder, he touched the sharp tips of the trident to the back of Oceanus's neck. "You're *our* prisoner now."

The claws went still. Oceanus turned his head, glancing fearfully at the trident. Whatever magic powers it had, he seemed scared of them. Of course, he would know just how powerful the trident was!

"C'mon!" Poseidon called to Zeus and Hades. The boys swam closer and grabbed on to the net. They climbed higher up Oceanus's back until they were alongside Poseidon. Now far above the water, Zeus summoned Bolt with a wave of his hand. Instantly the thunderbolt zoomed down and slid back under his belt.

"Onward!" Poseidon commanded Oceanus. "Take us to—um, land. Back to the dock we started from."

"You want me to give you a ride?" Oceanus laughed slyly. "Be glad to. But first you'll have to free me from this net."

"No way. How dumb do you think we are?" Hades shot back.

Oceanus pretended to think. "Well, on a scale of dumbness from one to ten, I'd say— Ow!"

Poseidon had interrupted him with a nudge from the sharp end of the golden trident. "Get moving!" he told the Titan.

Zeus could hardly believe it when Oceanus obeyed. But then again, the Titan didn't have much choice. Now that the magical trident was in Poseidon's hands, he was quickly learning how to use it.

The wind whistled in the boys' ears as Oceanus plowed across the sea toward Greece. They were moving faster than the seagulls flying overhead!

"What'll we do with him after we're back in Greece?" Hades shouted over the roar of the wind. "He'll be a danger to all Olympians if we let him go free."

"You got that right," Oceanus agreed before Zeus could reply.

"Stop listening!" Poseidon commanded. The boys huddled closer together, talking more quietly so the Titan wouldn't hear.

"We have to keep him tied up in this net," Zeus told his companions. "Until we can imprison him."

"But where'll we find a prison strong enough to hold him?" asked Hades.

Zeus's amulet twitched against his chest.

He jerked in surprise, almost losing his grip on the net.

"Ake-tip itan-Tip oo-tip artarus-Tip," the chip squeaked in its tiny voice.

Hades's dark eyes widened in surprise.

"Take Titan to Tartarus," Poseidon translated slowly. "Where's that?"

Zeus shrugged. "No clue." As Poseidon explained about Chip to Hades, Zeus lifted the amulet. He watched its black symbols rearrange themselves into squiggly lines and arrows.

"A map!" he said at last. "It must be showing us the route to Tartarus. And the dock's on the way."

The boys traveled on, following the map and giving Oceanus directions. They kept an eye out for Hera but didn't see her on land or sea. Zeus figured she'd be waiting for them. But when they reached the dock, she wasn't there.

 83

"Do you think King Cronus captured her again?" Poseidon asked anxiously.

"I didn't know you cared," teased Zeus. But the thought that Cronus or his Cronies might've nabbed her had him worried too.

"Just because I fight with her doesn't mean I want her to get recaptured," said Poseidon. He and Hera bickered a lot, but they *did* care about each other, Zeus realized. They'd grown up together and were both Olympians, after all. Whatever that meant.

"I vote we keep going," said Hades. "We can come back and search for her later."

"He's right," said Zeus. "We have to get Oceanus locked up. For everyone's safety. Including Hera's."

Once they were on land, Oceanus shed his serpent's tail for a pair of legs so that he could walk. "Where are you taking me?" he demanded.

"That's for us to know and for you to . . . uh . . . not know," said Poseidon. "Just march." He prodded Oceanus with the trident.

"Hey, watch it with that thing," the Titan complained. But he picked up his pace.

The boys continued to ride on his back, clinging to the net that covered his torso. Zeus checked the amulet now and then, making sure they stayed on course.

At the top of a winding road, they began to drop down through a thick forest. Eventually the forest gave way to an open valley.

"We should have waited for Hera," said Poseidon.

Zeus wondered if he was right. What if their decision to go on without Hera had been a bad one? On the other hand, she might never have shown up. He really hoped she was okay. Even if she did think he was one of Cronus's spies!

With that on his mind he turned toward Poseidon. "We have the trident now. So what was the big secret she was going to tell me once we got it?"

Poseidon shrugged. "I promised not to say. You'll have to ask her. If we ever see her again, that is."

"Hush," Hades hissed. With a finger to his lips he nodded across the valley to the hills on the other side. "Something's moving up there."

Overhearing, Oceanus halted. "He's right."

"Where?" asked Poseidon, shading his eyes.

Hades pointed, and Zeus's eyes followed his finger. Seconds later they all saw someone— or some*thing*—dart from behind a rock to the cover of a tree.

"Cronies?" Poseidon wondered aloud. He squinted at the place where the figure had been.

"Unfortunately, not," grumped Oceanus, who actually *liked* Cronies. "They wear armor."

"Then, what?" Zeus asked. The figure had moved so quickly, he hadn't had time to see it clearly. He was about to suggest they find a place to hide, just in case, when bloodcurdling yells filled the air.

"YAAAH!" All at once the hillside came alive with dozens of strange creatures. Strange because they had no heads. Instead their faces were smack in the middle of their chests!

Oceanus's eyes widened. "Cronus has let loose the first of the Creatures of Chaos! We're doomed!" His voice was a horrified wail.

"Creatures of Chaos?" Zeus echoed. "I remember that the king was talking about unleashing them, when I overheard him at his meeting in the forest with the other Titans." And Pythia had mentioned them in her prophecy. Hadn't she said the trident could defeat them?

"Don't you get it?" bellowed Oceanus.

"Those are Androphagoi coming at us. They're monsters! Man-eaters!" He shuddered. "They'll eat us alive!"

"YAAAH!" screamed the mouths in the middle of the monsters' chests. They had long, sharp teeth. Bone-crunching teeth! Brandishing clubs and spears, the beasts streamed downhill to the valley like big ants from an enormous anthill.

"It's an ambush!" shrieked Poseidon.

CHAPTER NINE

The Androphagoi

CEANUS TURNED AND RAN BACK THE
way they'd come. No need to prod him with
the trident to get him to move this time!

Soon they were back in the forest. The
Androphagoi were gaining on them. Zeus and
Poseidon had weapons, of course. But would
Poseidon's trident and Bolt really be a match
against an entire army of monsters? Zeus had
his doubts, despite the oracle's words.

As Oceanus passed a tree, Zeus leaped from his back, grabbing on to a limb. "Spread out and climb!" he called to the others. "We can pick them off one by one from high in the trees."

One of the monsters blew a dart. It zoomed past Zeus's shoulder as he scrambled up the tree trunk.

Poseidon and Hades followed his lead, also leaping onto trees. But Oceanus was much too big and heavy for any tree to hold him. And he couldn't have climbed very easily while wrapped in his net, anyway.

"Hide somewhere. But don't try to escape," Poseidon warned him.

Pulling Bolt from his belt, Zeus shouted "Large!" Sparking and sizzling with electricity, the zigzag bolt lengthened in midair.

"After them!" he commanded. "The Andro-phagoi, I mean," he added quickly.

Bolt flew toward the ground, then zipped through the forest. Soon high-pitched yips and unearthly grunts rang out as the thunderbolt struck one monster after another. Once they'd been zapped, the Androphagoi vanished into thin air. *Pop! Pop! Pop!*

They must be under some kind of enchantment, Zeus realized. Unfortunately, the remaining monsters didn't retreat. They just kept coming, one after another.

In a nearby tree Poseidon extended his trident downward. He speared the Androphagoi as they ran by. The trident's prongs flashed golden as they jabbed the beasts in their behinds. *Pop! Pop! Pop!* The creatures burst like bubbles.

But their numbers were huge and they continued to swarm through the forest. Things were looking bad.

Whack! Something shook the tree Zeus was

in. His foot slipped. He had to grab at a branch to keep from falling.

When he looked down, he saw one of the headless monsters on the ground directly below him. "YAAAH!" The face on its chest grinned up at him. Its jaws were slobbering. It swung its club again. *Whack!*

The tree trembled, but Zeus held on tight. The monster kept whacking, but the tree didn't fall. *Good thing the Androphagoi don't have saws,* Zeus thought. But, unfortunately, they did have legs. Abandoning his club, the monster below began to climb.

"Back off!" yelled Zeus. He went higher. But the Androphagos didn't give up. Putting two fingers to his lips, Zeus gave a loud whistle. "Here, Bolt. Come here, boy!" he called frantically.

Zeus could see the thunderbolt flashing here and there at the edge of the forest as it popped other monsters. But it must not have heard him. Looked like it was up to Zeus to save himself this time.

The monster was close now. Its razor-sharp teeth gleamed as it opened its mouth wide. "YAAAH!" it yelled. The Androphagoi sure did have a limited vocabulary.

By now Zeus had climbed to the top of the tree. There was no place to go except down. If he jumped, he'd only break his legs. Then he'd be boy meat for sure!

He felt hot breath on his ankle. The Androphagos snapped its jaws, trying to bite him. Why did practically everyone he'd met since leaving his cave in Crete want to eat him? Zeus wondered.

Sharp teeth clamped around the heel of his sandal. As the creature tugged on it, Zeus tried to kick it off. He lost his balance. His arms flailed in midair. Suddenly he and the monster were both falling.

Whump! The Androphagos landed on the ground on its back. *Thump!* Zeus landed on top of it. The monster had cushioned his fall!

Pop! It vanished, leaving Zeus sprawled on the ground alone.

Just then Bolt zoomed back. Zeus leaped up and brushed himself off. Bolt hovered in front of him. "About time you got here," he scolded. "I was almost mincemeat."

Bolt's glow dimmed. It stopped sparking. Zeus sighed. "Sorry. That wasn't fair. I know you were busy."

Looking around, he realized that the Androphagoi were completely gone. All of them. *Vanished.*

He smiled. "Good work, Bolt." At his praise the thunderbolt glowed brightly again. Making itself as small as a dagger, it slid under the belt at Zeus's waist.

Zeus gave it a little pat. "You're better than any old golden trident," he murmured. "I'll miss you when you go back to that Goose guy."

"We defeated them!" he called out to the others. Hades and Poseidon climbed down from their trees and joined him.

Having helped defeat the Androphagoi, Poseidon's trident now glowed with pride. It seemed as happy to be in Poseidon's possession as Bolt was in Zeus's.

The difference was that the trident really did belong to Poseidon now. Or so it seemed. The thunderbolt was only on loan to Zeus till Goose turned up to claim it.

"Wait! Where's Oceanus?" Poseidon asked, looking around.

Zeus had half-expected the Titan to slip away

while the battle raged. But they found him caught on a thorny branch, tangled up in his net.

After scrambling onto Oceanus's back, Poseidon used the sharp tips of the trident to cut Oceanus loose from the thorns. Zeus helped, using the thunderbolt to burn through the net's fibers.

"Cut my arms free while you're at it," Oceanus commanded in a sugary-sweet voice. "My claws are useless on it. I promise I won't try to escape."

"Don't believe him," Hades said, glancing at the Titan's clawed hands. "He's crossing his claws."

Poseidon glowered at Oceanus. "Swear on the trident."

The Titan glanced warily between Poseidon and the trident. Then he uncrossed his claws. "FINE!" he snarled, rolling his eyes. "I swear I won't escape." But no one noticed he was now crossing the claws on top of his head.

When they finished their work, the Titan's arms were free. The rest of the net still draped him like a cape, though. The boys clung to it as Oceanus began walking down into the valley again. They were all quiet for a time, just relieved to be alive.

"I never thought I'd say this about a fellow Titan," Oceanus muttered. "But it seems Cronus can't be trusted."

"We knew that a long time ago," muttered Zeus. "You just now figured it out?"

"Yeah, you've been following his orders!" Poseidon exclaimed.

"Like keeping me captive," Hades added.

"I had my reasons," Oceanus told them. "For one thing, Cronus is my king. I owe him allegiance. Besides, he told me you were plotting to overthrow him."

They were walking through a meadow now.

It was dotted with clumps of purple crocuses and other flowers. Ahead was a rocky hill they'd soon have to climb.

"Me?" said Hades. "I don't know how to overthrow anybody."

"Yeah, me either," said Poseidon. One of his arms was hooked through the net. With his free hand he twirled the golden trident like a baton.

Oceanus winced when Poseidon tossed the trident up into the air and almost missed it on the way down. "Careful! If you drop my trident, I'll—"

Poseidon's turquoise eyes flashed. "It's not yours now. It never really was. You stole it, didn't you!"

Zeus's ears pricked up. Was this true? How could Poseidon know that?

"Did not," Oceanus protested. "Cronus gave it to me years ago!"

"But he shouldn't have," Poseidon insisted. "It's mine." He glanced at Zeus. "When the sirens sang to us, I saw a vision of myself as a baby playing with this very trident. But it wasn't until I held it again that I knew it was truly mine."

Aha! thought Zeus. That explained Oceanus's wary glances at Poseidon. The Titan had known all along that the trident belonged to Poseidon!

"Did Cronus threaten to take back the trident if you didn't imprison me?" Hades guessed suddenly.

They'd reached the base of the hill. As Oceanus started to climb, he hung his head, then nodded. "To tell you the truth, he's always been sort of a bad apple. When we were young, he'd lie to get me in trouble. Just for fun." He clacked his crab claw hands. "He was always telling our parents I pinched him."

The three boys stared at the Titan in surprise. "Your parents?" Zeus said. "Does that mean you're—"

Oceanus nodded. "Brothers. Cronus is my *little* brother, to be exact." He paused before adding, "My *spoiled, bratty* little brother."

Whoa, thought Zeus. He'd often wished he had brothers and sisters, in addition to parents. But maybe being an "only" wasn't so bad!

Oceanus went on. "And now that he's unleashed the Creatures of Chaos, we're all doomed. Mortals and gods alike. He wants to rule over everyone. And Olympians are the only threat to his plan."

"Why are they a threat?" Zeus knew Hera and Poseidon suspected it had to do with magical powers. But maybe there was more to it than that.

"Because of the prophecy," Oceanus replied.

"What prophecy?" Zeus asked.

"The prophecy that an Olympian will rise up and lead other Olympians to defeat Cronus," Oceanus explained.

Before Zeus could get his mind around that, the ground below them began to rumble and shake.

"What now?" he wondered aloud.

CHAPTER TEN

The Oracle

QUICKLY THE BOYS SLID FROM THE NET to the ground. Zeus looked around wildly. Were more Androphagoi coming? Or an army of Cronies? Fortunately, he saw neither. He and the others jumped back in surprise as the earth split open in front of them.

"Pythia!" Zeus exclaimed as a cloud of glittery mist appeared. His companions gaped at

her. It probably wasn't every day that they saw magic this powerful. The boys were so intent on the oracle that they didn't notice when Oceanus began backing away.

The oracle's face, framed by long black hair, glowed within the mist. It was hard to see her eyes, though. Her glasses were fogged over as usual.

"Congratulations." The oracle smiled at the three boys. "The trident is now in the right hands—"

"Yes!" interrupted Poseidon. He pumped the trident up and down. "I knew it was mine!"

"Shh," said Zeus. "Let her finish."

"—and if used wisely, it will bring untold power, honor, and glory to the true god of the sea." She paused here, turning her foggy gaze on Poseidon.

"Stupefying starfish," he murmured in shock. "I'm the god of the sea!"

Well, that explains a lot, thought Zeus. Including why Oceanus seemed so afraid of Poseidon. It wasn't just to do with the trident. If Poseidon was god of the sea, then Oceanus was *beneath* him in rank.

"You have also defeated the first of the king's Creatures of Chaos," the oracle went on. Her gaze moved back to Zeus. "Well done. But your quest is not yet ended."

Excitement rose in Zeus at the possibility of more adventure. He leaned forward, listening intently. So did Poseidon and Hades.

"Next you must find the Helm of Darkness," Pythia informed them. "It rightfully belongs to the one who is lord of the Underworld. Find it and you will also find more of the persons you seek. Only, beware of the second of the king's Creatures of Chaos. For they are far more dangerous than the Androphagoi."

The second she stopped speaking, the mist vanished. So did she.

"Wait!" Zeus called out. "What's a Helm of Darkness? Who's the lord of the Underworld?"

But Pythia was long gone. Even the crack in the earth through which she'd appeared had vanished.

Hades frowned, mumbling worriedly. "More Creatures of Chaos? I don't like the sound of that."

"Me neither," said Poseidon. Then he looked around. "Hey! Oceanus is gone!" While their attention had been on the oracle, none of them had noticed the Titan slip away. *So much for promises. Maybe no Titan could be trusted!* thought Zeus.

As tall as Oceanus was, they still couldn't spot him anywhere. So they climbed to the top of the hill and gazed out across the valley. The Titan was nowhere to be seen.

"So much for trusting his word," said Hades. "I guess he's escaped."

"Do you think he heard Pythia?" Poseidon wondered. "Will he tell the king what she said?"

"I hope not. But there's no reason to go to Tartarus now," said Zeus. "Let's head for the Underworld instead. *Fast.* Before those half-giant Cronies can beat us there. Because if the Helm of Darkness belongs to the lord the Underworld, that's probably where we'll find it."

He checked Chip, figuring it would chart a new course. "Funny. It's still pointing the same way as before." He thumped it. No change.

Hades looked over his shoulder at the chip. "Maybe Tartarus is near the Underworld."

Zeus peered in the direction the arrow wanted them to go. In the distance he made out a huge marsh. A muddy, brown river snaked through it.

"All I know for sure is that we should head for that river," he said, pointing.

"Looks gloomy," said Poseidon. "And I bet it smells bad too."

Hades's face lit up. "Sounds perfect."

"Huh?" Zeus asked in surprise.

"He likes gloomy and stinky," Poseidon explained. "Like the inside of the king's belly."

Hades smiled dreamily. "Yeah."

What a weirdo, thought Zeus. He wondered what the other Olympians he hadn't yet met were like. And that made him think about Hera again. If all the Olympians were gods, then she'd be a goddess.

But goddess of *what*? Of being annoying, maybe?

That thought made him smile. She could be a pain at times. Still, he hoped she hadn't been eaten by the Androphagoi before they'd popped them all. Why, oh why, hadn't she waited for them like she'd said she would? Where was she now?

He should've asked Pythia when he'd had the chance. Not that she would've given him a straight answer. Oracles rarely did. But the next time Pythia appeared, he was going to get more out of her. Including why she was sending them on all these quests!

Still, crazy as it seemed, he looked forward to this new one. And one day soon perhaps all would be revealed.

Feeling destiny beckon, he started downhill toward the distant, gloomy river. "Follow me," he called to the other boys. And with that, they embarked on their next quest, heading for the Underworld. Together they would face whatever surprises and dangers awaited them there.

DON'T MISS THE NEXT ADVENTURE IN THE
HEROES IN TRAINING SERIES

AVAILABLE APRIL 2013

HOLUB   ICCRX
Holub, Joan.
Poseidon and the sea of fury /

CENTRAL LIBRARY   Friends of the
05/13   Houston Public Library